BLACKOUT

by Gary Lennon

A SAMUEL FRENCH ACTING EDITION

SAMUEL
FRENCH
FOUNDED 1830

New York Hollywood London Toronto

SAMUELFRENCH.COM

ISBN   978-0-573-66236-2   Printed in U.S.A.   #4923

MUSIC USE NOTE

IMPORTANT BILLING AND CREDIT
REQUIREMENTS

BLACKOUT was presented at the Harold Clurman Theater on November 11, 1991 under the direction of Ron Stetson with set design by Ron Kurash; lighting design by Zdenek Kriz; costumes by Clare Tattersall and stage managed by Sonya Smith.

The play was produced by the Second Generation Theater Company.

CAST:

HELEN	Jackie Bees
CARROLL	Jessica Bern
DEBBIE	Susan Boehm
KATHY	Jill Gatsby
JIM	Sam Grey
PATTY	Kelly Kane
JACK	Gary Lennon
BECKY	Lee Ann Martin
RACHEL	Nancy McDoniel
TIM	William Neish
KENT	Blair Tatton

TIME:
Christmas Eve. The present.

This play is dedicated to Gerome Ragni
for whom without his love, friendship and support
this play could not have been possible.

CAST OF CHARACTERS

JACK:
> *A man in his twenties. An orphan.*

TIM:
> *A man in his early twenties.*

DEBBIE:
> *A "rock and roller" in her twenties. Lots of unfocussed energy. Tough.*

PATTY:
> *A woman in her twenties.*

JIM:
> *A man in his fifties. Strong body with a boy's soul.*

CARROLL:
> *A beautiful live wire.*

HELEN:
> *A woman in her early thirties. Has seen it all.*

RACHEL:
> *A model whose prime has passed.*

BECKY:
> *A successful business woman.*

KENT:
> *A Wall Street puppy dog.*

KATHY:
> *A street urchin, disheveled, mid-twenties. She wears bell bottom jeans, and a hooded, zipped-up sweatshirt. She is obviously distressed.*

SETTING
An Alcoholics' Anonymous Meeting
at 8:00 p.m. on Christmas Eve. The present.

(The play opens with JACK speaking from a table at center stage. All others are sitting in folding chairs scattered in the room. The stage is bare except for the table and chairs. The twelve steps and twelve Tradition Signs of A.A. are hanging in the back with a Christmas wreath between them.)

(The play should be done without an intermission.)

(KATHY enters the room while JACK is in the middle of his qualification. She sits in between DEBBIE and PATTY. She is extremely self conscious and out of place.)

JACK. Hi, my name is Jack, and I'm an alcoholic.

EVERYONE. Hi, Jack!

JACK. Thank you. It's funny. I haven't been in this room in a long time. I haven't done this in a while. Qualified. I forget where to begin. Uh ... I'm so nervous. It's hard to believe I'm celebrating my seventh year of sobriety. It seems like yesterday I was a drunk. I guess I'm still a drunk, but a dry drunk. I never thought I had a problem with alcohol. People were always telling me that they thought I had a drinking problem. But being Irish, I thought they were crazy. I wasn't going to give in to that. Being a drunk. I was going to defy the tyranny of fact. One of my friends said, "I thing you're an alcoholic." I said, "No, not me." I thought an alcoholic was a bum, one of those guys sleeping in the streets in the Bowery. I was too young to be an alcoholic. I thought you at least had to be 40. Was I surprised when I hit bottom, and I woke up one morning in the street with somebody else's

7

clothes on, and I didn't know how I got there. I thought an
alcoholic had to drink every day of his life. I just drank every
other day. It's all denial. It's all the same. Excuses. No one
wants to admit it to themselves. My life has been so good
since I'm sober. I'll start at the beginning for the newcomers.
My advice is to stay with the program. It works. If I could
stop drinking, anybody could. I know everybody says that,
but it's true. I took my first drink when I was twelve, and it
seems like I never stopped. My brother got me drunk the first
time. It was beer. Then it was Boone's Farm Apple Wine. I
learned about sex through Boone's Farm. In P.S. 111 on a
ledge. It never seemed to get better than that. I was shy. The
wine loosened me up. You know what I mean. My father was
an alcoholic. He died of it. So this is a serious disease. He
died drunk. He died drunk with his face down in a puddle. He
could have lived if he wanted to. If he was sober. But he was
drunk. He died when I was little. And all I remember is that I
hated him. I can hardly remember his face, you know, but I
remember his smell. It was Jack Daniels. Me and my two
brothers took right after him. I don't think he meant all the
things he did. I don't think he wanted me to hate him, but he
could have at least told me he loved me once. No matter how
drunk he was. I hated the fights and the screaming and the
broken glass. He was a gangster. A tough guy. He robbed
banks and everything. He was in the paper. He did a lot of
time in jail. That's what they tell me. I know. Can you believe
it, me, coming from a gangster? It just doesn't fit. One of my
brothers died from trying to be just like him. They both spent
time in jail, too. I guess I didn't get to know him that well. I'm
going off track. Un. There are so many reasons why I began
to drink. Both of my parents were dead before I was thirteen.

I figured that was a good enough reason. When my mom died, I remember the night when they told me. I went out and got really drunk with my friends in the pack on 12th Avenue and 51st Street. We drank. I thought that if I drank so much, it would put me asleep, so that when I woke up, it wouldn't be real. She wouldn't be gone. I tried doing that for a long time. But it didn't work. She was gone. I remember the very next night I went down to the park again by myself. I brought a case with me. I drank, and there was this really bright star over the Chrysler Building, and it was watching me. I felt it. I know it was her, and I said to it, "I don't want to be like him. Don't worry, I'm not going to be like him," I promised. I don't want to be like him. I drank to be numb. Numb so I wouldn't feel the loss of them or feel the anger. The anger at someone or something for taking them away, because I didn't have a dad to teach me to play baseball, or teach me to fish, or teach me to be a man. I may have hated him, but I wanted him around. At least he was mine. Sometimes I'm angry because I missed out on my childhood. I had to grow up too fast. New York's a hard place when you're 14 years old and you have no family and you're fending for yourself. I missed out on things like Little League and snowball fights and someone telling me fairy tales before I went to bed. I wanted that. Things children should have. Instead, I was already fighting this disease called alcoholism. Instead I was in some hallway drinking, smoking cigarettes with people who could care less about me. They were your friends until someone else had a six pack. I drank to be happy. I drank to be sad. I drank to drink. I remember when I was really drunk one night there was a picture of me when I was 8 years old on my desk, and I looked at it, and I didn't know who it was. I didn't recognize that boy. I lost touch with him, and now being sober, I feel like I found him again. I drank all through high school. I used to have a bottle of scotch in my locker. I thought I was cool. I was kicked out twice, but they kept taking me back, because my grades were so good. I was smart. I was a functioning alcoholic. I had a 95.4 average. I don't know how it worked. After high school, I got jobs, but I didn't keep any because they would get in the way of my career of drinking. They were good paying jobs too. I should have a lot of money saved, or a nice apartment or something. I don't know where the money went. I guess I took a lot of cabs. Relationships were a joke. Alcoholics don't have relationships. They hold hostages. It's like, "You love me, don't you? You want to suffer with me, don't you?" I was married for four months, but it was a joke. I was drinking so much at the time that I was crazy. I was seeing this girl for six months, and she started to really drive me out of my mind. As you know, alcoholics are terrified of bring alone. So I was going to jump out the window or marry her. So I married her. I was stubborn. I never made love to anyone sober. I couldn't. I always had to be drunk. I just couldn't have sex sober. So quiet. It was too scary. It was too intimate. Just you and that one other person. I didn't have sex with someone sober until I was 20 years old, and I started having sex when I was 14. So there's six years of some good old Jack's drunk sex stories. When I finally did have sex sober, I felt so new at everything. It felt so bright. Like all these lights were on. I shook. I was clumsy. It was awful. I was awful. It was like do you really want to do this. My very last time being drunk was a blackout. That's when you don't remember what you do. It was a gin martini binge. Drinking did crazy things to me. I woke up in this afghan covered bed. I didn't know where I was or how I got there. I felt this strange sensation my body was going through. There was this smell in the room that was horrifying. Later I found out it was her shoes. I couldn't lift my head. I looked to the side of me and I saw this night table. On it was a clock. I was trying to make out the time when I saw this clear glass filled with water with something pink floating in it. I looked closer. It was someone's false teeth. Pink and white. And then I heard this sloshing sound underneath me. Sort of like llushshwwwahah. I felt someone tugging at me, down there. I looked down and there she was. This Spanish woman. She had knee high stockings on. She had her housedress over her head, and it was caught in her curlers and she had egg salad smeared all over her bare breasts, and somehow I knew I had something to do with it being there, because egg salad was my favorite sandwich. She was definitely a Ninth Avenue woman. She was trying to please me when I began to vomit. All of a sudden I was aware of the dampness of the bed. It was cold and wet. Then it started to register that one of us had an accident last night in our sleep and couldn't make it to the bathroom. I was hoping it was me. There were these huge wine stains on the sheets, like circus hoops. It was humiliating, but she seemed oblivious to it. I think it was her. She finally looked up and said, "I met you last night at the Blarney Stone next to McDonald's on 56th and 8th Avenue." That night I went back to AA. What I guess I'm really trying to say is that I'm grateful. I'm grateful for this room, and I'm grateful to be sober. When I first walked into this room seven years ago, I had a pint of Jack Daniels in my pocket and about a dollar fifty, and I was in ragged old clothes and I smelled just like my father. I came in and I sat in the back. I was scared. I didn't talk to anybody. I couldn't raise my hand to say my name. I thought all of you were crazy and derelicts and you all smoked so much. I thought, "Great. All these people are getting sober, and they'll die of lung cancer." All of you were saying such personal things. I was intimidated by your honesty. I said, "This place isn't for me." But I came back the next day and the next. I didn't have anywhere else to go. And the day after that and I kept coming back for 90 days. I came to a meeting every day, and the most important thing was I didn't drink. I didn't have to try and change my life in one day. I could do it one day at a time. I didn't say a word to any of you people, and you all shared your lives with me, telling your stories, and I thank you, because that's what kept me sober. Your stories. Just listening. You all loved me unconditionally, and you didn't even know me. You were all selfless. I love all of you, even the ones I don't know. The ones that just smiled at me and made me feel welcomed in the room. You all gave me the love that I was looking for. And now, you know what? Every night at seven o'clock, I look out my window and I look up at that same star over the Chrysler Building, and I'm not drinking. And somehow I know she has something to do with it, and it makes her feel good! Because I know it makes me feel good! The most important thing being sober has done for me is helping me know who I am! Who Jack is! When I was drinking I didn't know who I was. I had spent all those years developing into a drunk person who didn't know himself. Who I didn't like. When I got sober, I asked myself, "Who are you? What makes you tick? How do you feel about that?" It's hard to be honest with yourself sometimes. But you know what? I loved asking those questions, and finding out all the answers. And I'm still asking. And I'll ask till the day I die. So many people go around not knowing who they really are. They're afraid to ask. The answers might scare them. It's hard to take that extra moment to take a long look in the mirror and confront yourself. Do it! It's worth it. It's a joy to live your life with a sense of truth. You know what the best part of being sober is? It's being able to go out with someone at night and being able to see them the next day without being humiliated about what you did or said the night before. Just the simple fact that you can look them in the face and say, "Hi." It's taken my 24 years to find the definition of the words integrity, honesty, friendship and love, and I learned them through you. Thank you. Merry Christmas, everybody. I've taken up a lot of time. It's good to be here tonight. Thanks. Lets open it up, on this fine night ... we'll go around in a circle if you don't want to speak. Pass ... Tim ... you start.

TIM. Hi my name is Tim and I'm an alcoholic.

ALL. Hi Tim.

TIM. It's always good to hear you speak Jack. I'm trying to make a good Christmas for myself, but it's hard. Right now I'm supposed to be on a plane, on my way home to visit my parents, but this afternoon I chickened out. I'm glad I stayed and came here. I identified with a lot of what Jack said. Especially about his father. Even though our backgrounds are very different, I understood a lot of it. I grew up in a small town outside of Concord, New Hampshire. My father was the coach of our high school football team. He was also sort of the town drunk, and hero. Very macho. I started drinking very young, too. For different reasons. Just like Jack. I think I was about fourteen or fifteen. I don't remember exactly. I drank to cover up my inadequacies which my father pointed out as

often as he could. From early on, I knew I was different. I
wasn't like the other kids. I tried, but it just seemed fake. As
a kid, I always had this feeling I just didn't fit in. You know,
I never lost that feeling until I got sober. I couldn't wait to get
out of New Hampshire. I tried doing all the things my father
wanted me to. I tried to get good grades. I tried going out for
the football team, even thought I was painfully thin. Even my
older brother, who was the quarterback, tried to save me from
that humiliation, but my father made me try. It just didn't
work out. I tried going out with the girls my brother set me up
with, but I knew inside it just wasn't happening. I was
different and I knew it. It wasn't like I was a geek or the kids
made fun of me or anything. I mean you couldn't tell I was
different, like ... whatever that means ... I mean I tried to fit
in. What I'm trying to say is that all the guys treated me like
one of the guys, but I knew. I mean I tried being like them. I
mean ... I wore ... you know ... um. Baseball caps and sweat
pants and I tried talking really loud like them ... like you
know ... "Hey you! Get over here. How ya doin'!!? What's
up!? Ecay! And I tried watching basketball games at home ...
and you know put it up really loud and scream and stuff
yeah!! All right!! ... and I tried drinking dark beer, but I don't
know ... it just didn't feel natural to me. I felt like I was this
imposter. I knew I was lying and I didn't want to. I wanted to
be able to just be myself. So I drank. And that way I could be
one of them. I could try and be this person they wanted me to
be. I went out with this girl for two years and it was fine. We
had fun. We drank. We had sex. It was fine, but it didn't have
that spark, the fire that I heard it was supposed to have. And
I knew it made my brother and father happy, so I did it. Then
when I was a junior, me and my oldest brother Joe's best

friend, Tom, and I got drunk in our basement. We touched each other, and we kissed and it felt right to me. I don't know, It was sort of beautiful, I guess. But that spark still was missing. Needless to say, I spent a lot of time with Tom after that. And my father was happy that I was spending so much time with Tom, because Tom was such a man. He was on the football team and everything. He was a regular guy. Anyway, it didn't last long, and I drank a lot more after that. I had a taste for something, and I wanted more. I was angry. I started getting very violent when I was drunk. I got my front teeth knocked out in fight. I put my hand through plate glass windows. I wanted out of New Hampshire. I think my father and brother always knew about me, but they wouldn't say it. After high school, I told them I was moving to New York. They thought I was crazy. They said they refused to pay my tuition at NYU. I'd have to do it by myself. There was one person who was my saving grace when I was a kid, and that was my Aunt Katie. She was the one who always made me feel like I was good enough, just the way I am. She helped me make the move and always stood by my decisions, no matter how alcohol influenced they were. When I got to New York, I discovered drugs, Yes! and I loved them. They made me feel ... I got totally involved in the whole scene and I was ugly and I was crazy for a long time. I cut my family off except for Aunt Katie for a few years. I found a new sense of freedom and like most freedoms I abused it. I found a lot of sex, drugs, but no sparks. After a while, drugs and alcohol stopped working for me. They didn't make me happy anymore. I was always sad and alone, with all these people in New York, I was alone. I looked like shit. I isolated myself in this big city. All of a sudden, I had this urge. This need for my family. I missed them. My Aunt Katie always wrote to me and kept me informed about what was going on in my family. I had learned that my brother Joe had been arrested a few times for drunk driving and beating his wife. That assured me that he was drinking as much as me. She told me my mom was fine and Dad had been asking about me. Oh, yeah. She wrote me, that the <u>town</u> scandal was, "Do you remember Tom, your brother Joe's friend? Well, he has left his wife for a man." No, not Tom! I was happy for him, actually, and I was secretly hoping someday I'd find someone. I hardly remember the last year of my drinking. I can tell you that I didn't finish college, and I can tell you that the job that I had was in some restaurant in the village. I can't remember its name. I think ... I think I blocked the name out of my mind totally. I won't even walk down Sullivan Street. I think it was on Sullivan Street. I have such a block against it because that's the last place I remember being before waking up on the detox floor. I had a BLACKOUT. I sort of remember bits and parts. I remember getting Quaaludes and drinking Stoli at some dance bar. I knew I had to work the next day at the restaurant so I got some coke to keep me up. It didn't work. Between the coke, the ludes and the Stoli, I was anaesthetized. The rest of the story the owner of the restaurant tole me in the hospital, even though I begged him not to. I must have been afraid I wouldn't make it to work. So instead of going home after the bar, I went and slept in front of the gates at the restaurant. I wanted to make sure I was on time. I hated being late. That makes sense. When the owner came to open up, he found me curled up with a bottle of Stoli in my arms, asleep. He said he thought I was a bum, because of the smell. When he went to pick me up, he saw that I had shit and urinated in my pants. I must have gotten into a fight or fell, because there were cuts over my eyes and on my chin. He brought me back into the bathroom and washed me up. This little old Italian man. He was an angel. When two of the other waiters came in, they brought me to the detox. I shook for two days straight. They gave me medication to stabilize me. How did it get so bad so fast? I wasn't aware of the progression. When the guys in the group at detox heard my story, they made a nickname up for me. STP Short for Shit The Pants! You can laugh. It's ok. I do. It's funny. They taught me not to take myself too seriously. You know that slogan, "This too shall pass." And it did. It's good to remember there are a lot of people out there who are less fortunate than me. People who don't make it to the program. People who die trying to get sober. I always try to laugh with life as much as I can. It makes it a lot easier. While I was in there, I wrote to my Aunt Katie. I asked her to tell my parents where I was. I missed them. I wanted to come home for a visit when I got out. I wanted to stop running from them, from myself and from my problems. I decided I was going to tell them that I was different, and that it wasn't bad and it's not a disease and that I want them to love me still in spite of it. I'm not a pervert. I don't have sex with strangers in dark rooms. I'm a loving human being. I make love fully and passionately just like you do. I feel love just as strongly as you do. I need it as much as you do. I felt like if I could finally say it and mean it, then I could stop running from it, from relationships, from friends. I always felt like if my friends knew I was different, they wouldn't like me. In detox, I learned that saying, that, you know, "Hi, my name is Tim and I'm an alcoholic" is equally as hard to say as "Hi, my name is Tom and I'm ... different" and not feel ashamed of it.

I still have a hard time saying that three letter word. It's stupid. I still have a hard time saying it. When I got out, I did tell my parents and my brother and Aunt Katie, and you know what, they weren't shocked. I mean everything's not great now, but at least I've done my part of it. I told them. It's up to them now. I can tell my Dad still feels weird with me when we are alone. But that's OK. There is this tension in the room. Or if we are at dinner and our knees hit underneath the table, there's an awkward silence and there's this face he makes. What hurts is the silence in the room when we're alone. He avoids looking into my eyes. Because he knows the truth. He remembers. He sees it. I know he remembers what we did when he was drunk. He's just ashamed. That's why he avoids my eyes, because he sees it in them. I remember he called it a special game just between us. He wasn't that drunk. He planned it out. I remember the first time it happened. It was a Saturday morning and no one was home except me. I remember it was a Saturday, because I was watching my favorite cartoon, and I was laughing. It was the Christmas weekend. He came into my room and he stood by the front of the bed. He was drunk. He said he wanted to play with me, and I was surprised because he never wanted to play with me. It was always Joe. Then he said he wanted me to touch him, and I did, and I did because I wanted him to love me. That's why I did it. It happened a lot when he was drunk, and then it stopped. He just stopped doing it. I want to confront him about it, ya know, but when I look at his face, I see this old man. This sad old man, living a lie all these years, and I feel sorry for him, and I know he's punished himself all this time, and there's nothing that I could do or say that could make a difference. His eyes whisper to me, they say one word. They

say, "Don't!" So I don't. I just find it ironic that they are all
ashamed of me, and he's the hero ... I should have played
football, I guess. I know that incest is as common in alcoholic
families as a cow is to India, but just like that saying, "Shit
Happens", when it happens to you, you can't help but ask
why. A friend of mine, a girl, who was a victim of incest as a
child said when she fully realized her anger as an adult, she
wanted to go home and nail his balls to the floor, put a pair of
scissors in his hand and set the house on fire. I don't feel that
anger anymore. It just hurts sometimes. My brother has
gotten drunk a few times and called me in New York to tell
me I'm a faggot, and I was like ... oh really ... wow thanks.
I'm really glad you felt you had to share that with me did you
call live at Five and give them the New News Bulletin? ...
He's threatened to kill me and put me out of my misery. And
then I'll get a phone call from him a week later at three
o'clock in the morning, drunk, crying. Telling me how much
he loves his little brother. It's OK. It hurts sometimes. I miss
his friendship a little. I guess he's not ready. I pray for him
though, that he gets help with his drinking. Because I love
him. I love Mom, too. The person who was the best about it
was my Aunt Katie. She just said, "Follow your heart and all
of your dreams will come true." She just died last month, and
I miss her more than anything. I could really use her help in
this time of sobriety. I miss her not judging me. I miss her
support. I miss her letters telling me to be careful in the big
city. Whenever I had a fight with somebody, I'd always call
my Aunt Katie, and she'd make everything all right. When I
was a kid, I'd run over to her house on the hill, crying, if I had
a fight with my mom. She'd get these two chilled glasses
from the ice box. They had her initials on them, K.M. She'd

get them and she'd pour us two full glasses of homemade lemonade and tell me some funny story, and then everything would be alright. My mom doesn't want anything to do with me or my perverted way of living. She said I'm sick. She sees me as a failure because I won't give her a grandson. Personally I think she's very goal oriented. I decided I'm not going home for Christmas this year. Last year was just too weird. My mother didn't say a word to me. It's OK ... my mom ... She sat there in a rocking chair with her dog, Mush, in her lap and cradled him like a baby and said, "This is the only grandson I'll have, and he has four legs." Staring at me. I don't think I want to put up with that again this year. I miss them, though. I sent them a card. Kill them with kindness. There are a lot of things not settled in my life but I'm not going to drink over them. I don't feel inadequate anymore. I feel complete. I'm not going backward. I'm going forward. In big steps. I've learned I'm fine just the way I am. I don't have to drink. Things are good in my life right now. The only thing missing in my life is someone to share all of God's wonder with. I know now that includes me, too! I'm looking for the sparks ... but I don't know, ever since I've been a kid fireworks have made me blink. All in time. Easy does it. Thanks for letting me share. I needed to be here today. Merry Christmas.

(Blackout)
(Lights up on ...)

CARROLL. I'm feeling a little hostile today. I'm supposed to be at a very fashionable crowded party right now, but I decided not to go ... because I hate people today. So instead I decided to come here and share that with you ... the funny thing is I used to like people before I got sober and became aware of all their faults. I used to live to go out, but not since I'm sober. I feel like I act like I'm a ninety-nine year old woman with cataracts lately ... Oh. I don't know ... I got a phone call today ... No ... I was the type of creature who was out every night. I was so afraid I would miss something if I stayed in, so I went to every party, every club I could. Some nights I'd hit six, seven different places. I knew somebody, somewhere was having fun, and I was determined to find them ... and when I found them I was going to tell them off for not inviting me. I was so afraid of missing out on a good time. The fact is I wouldn't have known a good time if it hit me in the face. I was just afraid if I didn't go out, that that would be the night everybody would have a great time ... and then I'd be passed. So I kept trying, for years ... Nobody could say I gave up easy. Nobody could call me a quitter ... You ever put a shot glass up to your eye and look through it? Well, that's how I saw the world the whole time I drank. I just felt like there was this long murky wall up between me and everybody else. There's also like this prism effect. You could see things many different ways, many different colors and shapes, and I liked that, because if anything went wrong, I could justify it by how I saw it. I could rationalize and explain my way out of everything. I got into a lot of arguments at bars. I was a loud drunk. I used to tell stories and jokes real loud into people's ears. Until they ran from me. You could usually bet on it, that by the end of the night someone would call me a drunk. I can't tell you how insulted I was. I would then ask if they wanted to step outside and discuss this. My Bronx style. A fist fight. Of Course. You can take the girl out of the Bronx, but you can't take the Bronx out of the girl. Believe me, I'm trying. I should've known I was an alcoholic just by the name of the bars I drank in. Let's see they were The Last Stop. The Wrong Number, The Tunnel, and The Terminal, oh yeah and how could I forget Blarney Stone. The whole time I drank I accomplished nothing. When I got sober the only think I could put on my resume was Regular at McHale's Tavern. I was a sight ... When somebody called me a drunk, I immediately retaliated by screaming to the bartender and telling him to please stop serving that person, because obviously they couldn't handle their drink ... then I would quietly ask the bartender to ask that party to leave. I didn't have a regular bar that I went to all the time, for reasons I've already disclosed. Usually after about two weeks, I was embarrassed enough not to go back ... uh ... there was this awful joke I used to tell all the time. I was sort of known for it. I don't know where I got it from. It was ... um ... I told it very loud of course ... "What do you do with a dog with no legs?" ... pause ... then loudly ... "Take it for a drag." I don't understand why, but I thought it was a riot when I was drunk ... Um ... I quickly found out that when men drank, their main objective was, as Spike Lee would say, "Was to hide the salami." I just as quickly found out that when I drank, my main objective was to help them hide the salami. I'd like to make believe that that doesn't bother me, but it does. Some people may think that was too personal to share, but I feel I have to share that in order to get rid of it. I'm not proud of it, but it's part of who I am or was or something. When I got really drunk, I used to lie. I pretended I was other people. Unconsciously of course. I used to pretend I was lots of people. The most famous being Diane Von Furstenberg. Can you imagine it? Me? I used to get really drunk and go around introducing myself as Diane Von Furstenburg. When people began pointing out to me that I wasn't her, I became irate. I began to cry. Not just cry, but scream crying all over the bar. Yelling at the top of my lungs that I was Diane Von Furstenburg, that people were always accusing me of lying and how dare they doubt my sincerity. My namesake. That I resented them for it. Then someone would sit me down and get me some coffee and point out that I had red hair and blue eyes. I insisted on showing them my Diane Von Furstenburg birthmark I didn't have. I was out of my mind. I guess I hated being myself so much, I had to make believe I was someone else to get through it ... I was so many people. I told people I had butlers and chauffeurs and all kinds of stuff. I remember I lived on 73rd and York for a while. I lived in this five flight tenement walk-up and across the street from me was this beautiful building with a doorman and a fountain. It was forty stories high. I had such low self-esteem ... it wasn't like the Bronx. It never failed. Whenever I had a few drinks in me, I would take a taxi home and tell the driver to leave me off in the driveway of the beautiful high rise. The doorman would open the door for me, I would get out, say hi and wait for the taxi to take off. Then the doorman would look at me strange. I would say something, and then dart across the street to my sad little apartment. Eventually I lost that apartment. I moved around so much when I was drinking. My life was in two big Hefty bags. Hefty bags saved me. They went wherever I went. I was always sleeping on some friend's kitchen floor. At the time, I thought I was very fashionable. I thought of myself as this "Holly Golightly" type. This free spirit. I was wrong, of course. I was a glamorized bag lady is what I was.

I was very proud of those two Hefty bags. They had everything I needed in them. My clothes, some books, make-up, everything. I thought I was very neat. I had everything in order in those bags. God damn it! What is it about drinking that brings that "sex" thing out in all of us? I went through this period where I was only attracted to men in uniform ... you know, buy boys, sanitation workers, post office employees, the best. I could go on, but I won't. I'll never forget one morning when I was coming home from being out all night. The sanitation workers were taking the garbage from the front of the building of where I was staying and I took ... oh, I can't ... forget it. It's just awful ... Actually he wasn't bad. So anyway after a while, I got tired of sleeping on people's floors. So I got myself a job and an apartment. I got myself a restaurant job. I quickly found out that I could drink for free at my job. A fantastic benefit. Who the hell needs health insurance, anyway. I worked in restaurants for a while. I used to drink a little bit all through the night. So I was feeling pretty good working. Real friendly. I worked at this place where a lot of celebrities came, and as a result of my drinking, I slept with a lot of them. Actors, directors, producers, even some writers. I was moving up. I was very impressionable. I was young. They'd ask me to meet them when I got off, and I did. Hotel rooms. I guess I was trying to feel important through them. I did that with men a lot. I was as good as the man I was sleeping with. I had no self worth. Forget about self-respect or self-esteem. At the time, I didn't think I was being used by them. I didn't feel cheap. I didn't feel ... like they were getting over on me. I didn't feel like this barfly BIMBO, but I was. I thought at the time I was this young girl having an adventure. A good time, I called it. I can tell you now, it wasn't fun. There's this one guy that still calls. You'd know him if I said his name. He's a very famous director, actor, producer, whatever. Anyway, that's not important. I was with him a lot. Sometimes when I was drunk, he'd make me ... no, he didn't make me ... I'd do things with him and his friends. One night, I was drunk, and I was at his hotel room. He was drunk, too. He was treating me particularly bad that evening, and I left. When I got home, I got this dirty phone call from him, and I hung up. He called back, and I took the phone off the hook. I didn't hear from him for a while. I know, can you believe it? What an asshole, like he doesn't have anything else better to do, but bother me. Go direct something for Christ's sake! I wish he would just stop calling ... I know it's him. It's his voice. I say his name, and I ask for him to talk to me normal, but he won't ... He tells me what I did. It didn't get to me when I was drinking, but since I'm sober ... I don't know, it just drives me crazy ... He keeps saying things I did with him and his friends when I was drunk, and I don't want to hear them. I don't want to remember them. I want to make believe that's all gone. That's not me anymore. I'm not like that ... I have to talk about these personal things, because I want to wash out the demons that drove me to drink. I want to confront my innermost fears and conquer them. I think that maybe if I face them, they'll no longer exist. I want to purge myself from my dark secrets, from the men, the phone calls. The past. I don't want to carry them around with me anymore. All that extra baggage. It's garbage. Every time I face something new, I feel like this burden has been lifted from me. I feel a little cleaner. I want to feel clean. I want to forget it happened. It was like there were two distinct different personalities in me. When I drank,

there was one, and now that I'm sober, there's a different one.
It's like the difference bet \een Betsy Johnson and Laura
Ashley. A lot of people, mostly my old friends, don't think of
me as a free spirit anymore, they think I take life too
seriously, but they're wrong. I'm freer than ever. I don't live
out of bags anymore. I've actually put them away ... in my
very own dresser drawers. I iron now. I iron my own clothes.
That's a big deal for me. I still get all those alcoholic impulses
to do irrational things, but the difference is, now I just
acknowledge them, and I don't act on them. I realize that all
that time I spent searching for something in others in motion,
I can find by just being still ... As of now, I'm done with men
for a while ... Since I've been sober, I haven't dated anybody
seriously, and I think it's because I know I'm not ready ... But
I can't help feeling like I haven't had sex since platform shoes
were in style and the Beatles were climbing the charts ... but
it's alright ... I'm sort of having this romance with myself, and
it's nice. I'm taking care of myself for the first time in my life.
I'm fulfilling my own wants and needs, and it feels good,
being responsible. Living in one place. I'm not self-
destructive anymore. I've also stopped thinking that any
relationship is better than no relationship. I don't think I
should be in a relationship for a while. I won't be good to
anybody unless I'm good to myself first. When I just got
sober there was this one guy that I was really crazy about. I
was nuts about him. It was early in my sobriety, and he
became my obsession. I had given up alcohol, but he had
become my drug. I lost myself in him. Basically I turned my
life over to him to do whatever he wanted to do with it. I gave
him all my power, and he didn't treat me great. He confirmed
all my fears and insecurities, and of course that made me

more attracted to him. One morning when I woke up next to him I realized my life had become a hobby, and even though I was sober I was in bad shape. It was sort of like waking up each morning and saying to him, "Hi, how am I doing today? Would you like to tell me how I feel, because I haven't got a clue." It was hard to let go of that misery, but I ended it. I just have to stay clear or men for a while. I feel like God's telling me I'm not old enough to have a boyfriend yet, and that's okay for now. I just want to make sure I'm showing up for life ... thanks.

(KATHY is eagerly waving her hand.)

KATHY. *(She is having a hard time speaking)* Hi ... Umm ... this is my first time ... I am ... I ... My name is Kathy ... I don't know what to do. *(Long pause. She nods her head, no)* ... I don't know if I'm ... um ... I don't wanna talk. Really, okay?

(She puts her head down. JACK calls on someone else.)

JACK. Patty.
PATTY. Hi my name is Patty, and I am an alcoholic.
ALL. Hi Patty.
PATTY. This is probably one of the hardest days of the year to stay sober. Christmas Eve. All the normal people seem happy. Everyone's smiling. Bells are ringing. Children everywhere. Johnny Mathis and Andy Williams are singing their hearts out. Those songs. Everywhere I look I see Bing Crosby ... and then I hear "White Christmas". If I watch Miracle on 34th Street, they'll have to put me in a coffin. Last

night I stayed up really late and watched <u>The Bells of St. Mary's</u>, and I was hysterical. I've been a mess all day. My playing Handel's "Messiah" all morning didn't help. I can't shale this feeling. I'm having a hard time not drinking today. On my way to this meeting, I passed a bar I used to go to all the time, and I came very close to going in. I don't know what it is. I don't know what it is, most days I'm fine, but lately ... I think it's the holidays. All that Christmas cheer is getting me down. I decided I'm not going home for the holidays. It's too painful. All my drunk uncles sitting around drooling in brogue. Every year, my father sings the worst drunken version of "Danny Boy" I ever heard. It never fails He makes me sit on his lap until he finishes it, and then he starts crying, and I'm sitting there and I don't know what to do. It's a strange moment. When I was drinking, I would try to harmonize with him and cry along with him. We made a sad couple. And then my mother always takes out this family slide show of how I ruined her life and proceeds to humiliate me by showing it to the entire family. It gets messy. There it is up on the screen: the progression of my drinking career in big black and white slides. The deterioration of my spirit. "There's Patty at the punch bowl." "There's Patty in the punch bowl." "There's Patty in her bra." "Patty, how could you have done that, you embarrassed us." My mother is a martyr. She's the type of woman who thinks she's cornered the market on pain and humiliation. She has a monopoly on it, and she reminds me every chance she gets. She's always called me selfish. I don't know why. She says the first word that came out of my mouth when I was a baby was 'me' ... and the second word was 'mine'. She says I always wanted to be the center of attention ... well, in a way she's right. When

I got drunk, I became a real exhibitionist. I hit on anything that could walk. I always got this incredible urge to take off my clothes. It didn't matter where I was ... it didn't matter where I was. I did it in bars, Lexington Avenue, First, Third Avenue, girlfriends' parties. Needless to say, I got a bad reputation. Anyway, Christmas at home doesn't seem to appeal to me this year. The holidays always get me down. The last time I had a blackout was two years ago on Christmas Eve. It was at my parents' house. The whole family was there. I was drinking Seven & 7s with my seventeen year old niece and her boyfriend, Bob. After about nine Seven & 7s, I wound up in the garage naked, making out with Bob. I was trying to pull his pants down when Barbara came in. It was more like a brownout, because I vaguely remember seeing some of it. I remember my drink was resting on the hood of my father's car. Barbara started screaming at me. She was crying and she smacked me and knocked over my drink. I remember I started screaming back at her because she knocked my drink over! What the hell was wrong with her?! All the screaming got the family's attention, and they came out to the garage. They were all there – my mother, my father. Just staring at me, naked. Bare. All my little nephews were giggling at seeing me naked. Christmas day, my father took me aside and asked me if I would leave. It was too uncomfortable for the rest of the family. I used to be Barbara's favorite aunt, and now she doesn't talk to me. My sister, either. I didn't mean it. I could say that until I'm blue in the face, but it doesn't change what I did. They're not very forgiving. I really shouldn't say this, but I want to drink right now so bad. More than anything. I'm praying to God for this feeling to go away. I took off work today, because I knew I couldn't ... couldn't make it through without a drink. I called my sponsor, and she said get to a meeting. So I'm here. I want to be happy so bad. I want to forget two years ago. I want this to be a Merry Christmas. I wasn't going to get a tree, but I went out last night in the snow at midnight and I got one. Just a little one. They were selling them on Ninth Avenue and 23rd Street. I carried it home and I set it up on this table. I put a white cloth underneath it. I didn't put any balls or lights on it. I just left it bare. I don't know why, but that little Christmas tree standing there <u>bare</u> reminded me of myself, and I cried. It reminded me of me bare. I feel like for the last year I've been walking through mud fighting this losing battle. I feel half alive today, and I feel like that one drink would make me complete. I know it's the wrong thing for me, but I can't get it out of my mind. I want to find the new lights in my life. I want to invite anybody who doesn't have anywhere to go for Christmas to come to my place and help me decorate my tree. I don't want it to be bare. I'd appreciate it. We can listen to carols and have hot cider and eat cookies and stay sober together, go into sugar shock ... and you can help me forget. It's funny, but it's harder to forget than to remember. I just want to have a Merry Christmas. I really wanted to talk to my sister before the holidays ended. I didn't know if I should call. I prayed to God for his guidance. I turned it all over to a higher power. Guess what, yesterday my sister called me and said she wanted to see me. She said after the first.

(Blackout)

DEBBIE. Yeah. I just wanna say, I'm grateful I'm here and not drunk under some Christmas tree on Flatbush

Avenue. Thanks ... that's it. Oh, wait a minute. My name is Debbie, and I'm an alcoholic and a major drug addict. I'm serious. You can check me in under grateful. Oh, I guess i should tell you something about myself. I have a hard time sharing, but once you get me started, I can't stop ... I was born a long, long time ago, in a far away place called Brooklyn and got married in Las Vegas. How I got there, I don't know. I was in a blackout. I was married for six weeks. I was nineteen years old. I was married to this guy named Wild Bob! That was his full name. Wild Bob. So I guess I was Mrs. Wild Bob. Welcome to my life! Do you, Debbie, take Wild Bob to be your lawfully wedded husband? I do. I can't believe I said I do. He was a rock musician, like Gregg Allman. What could I do? I was a sucker for musicians. I went on tour with him for six weeks. When the tour ended, I got it annulled. Thank God I only did it once. I came right back to New York. My drinking took me across America and back. I was a rock and roll groupie. I was Pamela de Barres of CBGBs and Max's Kansas City. I only liked men with hair longer than mine. I was into the whole downtown scene. East Village and everything. I loved the music and the bands. It just went together with the drinking. Tequila, shots. Drugs. I feel like I was dating Jose Cuervo. I never had a job that whole time. I just lived off of people's generosity. I slept wherever I found myself. I could always crash at my parents' house if worse came to worse. My parents were always good to me, too. I started the whole drinking thing myself. Both of the parents don't drink. I was just a rebel. What is it about humans that when people tell us to do something, we automatically choose to do the direct opposite. Go to school. I dropped out. Don't drink. I drank! Watch out for boys! Forget about it. I don't know. I've been in and out of these rooms four or five times now. It took me two and a half years to get 90 <u>days</u> of sobriety ... that's a lot of drinking. I've always done the direct opposite of what's good for me. I've gone through life sabotaging myself. I was told alcohol was like a mine field to me, and I freely walked right through it. Making sure I hit all of the mines. Why is there always so much excitement in danger? I think I drank because I was pissed off I didn't grow up in the sixties, and party with Janis Joplin. You know what I mean. Everyone had long hair. The music was great. Peace, love, the clothes. I don't know. I think I was trying to relive the sixties in the eighties, and it just didn't work out for me. I think it's great that people can drink socially, and people do. But I can't. I wanted to be Janis Joplin so bad. So bad. She was great. Maybe instead of following those other groups, I should have started my own. No, I don't think so. I can't sing. But that doesn't stop half of them, right? I don't have a lot of regrets for what I did. Sometimes I wish I would of went to college instead of Studio 54, but not alot, ehh. Whatever I did, I did. I had a good time doing it, and now it's over. Whatever I did it got me to where I am now, and I like that. I don't hang on to the past, that's boring. That's why I hate that song on New Year's Eve. That Guy Lombardo shit. Forget about it. Pick up, move on. I had my fun, and I'm going to have a lot more. Sober. Things change. Face it. Wake up. Stop moaning. When I first came into these rooms and I heard all of you people complaining and moaning. I thought, oh God all these people need is a good stiff drink. Let them get drunk fa Christ's sakes. Of course I was wrong. Then I heard all these grateful people. I'm grateful for this I'm grateful for that. I'm positive. I'm wonderful. It made me want to throw up. I still get mixed feelings sometimes, but I keep coming back. I mean, sometimes I feel like yelling at all of you and tell ya that I think you all read one self help book too many, and then there are the times when I'm down and all of you are there for me, and I just wanna get down on my knees and kiss your toes, forever ... ya know what I mean. I'm a strange bird. I was born weird. I don't know. Whenever I had a problem, people kept telling me trust in God, don't worry turn it over to God. Trust, turn it over to God, and I wanted to trust in God but being from Brooklyn, I kept thinking that God was gonna rip me off. Now I don't though. I trust. I turn it over. I don't know. It works. Sometimes people say to me, Why are you angry all the time? Why you look to angry? And I have to tell them, Hey I'm not angry. This is how I look. This is it. This is the mug God gave me, but the same people keep asking me why am I angry, and that makes me angry. I've had to start doing physical things to release the stress. I've gotten into sports now. Watching them. I love NFL football. Can you believe it? Me? I especially like Keith Millard on the Minnesota Vikings. He's great. He's my favorite. Howie Long's not bad, either. He plays for the Los Angeles Raiders. Uniforms again. Bo Jackson's great, too. A friend of mine got me a ticket to the Pro Bowl for a Christmas gift. It's in Hawaii, and I'm going. I can't wait. It's in January. I'm home every Monday night. Nine o'clock, channel seven. Monday Night Football with Frank, Don and Al, I take the phone off the hook, make some popcorn, kick my feet up and that's it ... There's two games on Sundays, too, so I stay in. Sometimes ESPN has one on at eight, so then there's three games. It's fun. I'm starting to get into college football, too. It's on all day Saturday. So my weekends are pretty much booked.

There was really stiff competition for the Heisman trophy this year. I'm obsessive about most things I do. If I start working out, I want to be a bodybuilder. If I go on a diet, I want to lose fifty pounds even if I don't have to. When I say no potato chips, I mean no potato chips. I want results fast. I have no patience. I don't enjoy the process of things. I have to learn how to enjoy the process. Like the process of recovery. I want five years now. I got to take it easy. I have to learn how to relax. Football relaxes me. Next year I'm gonna get season tickets for the Giants' games. This addictive personality of mine gets me in trouble. Also I've become political for the first time in my life. I'm waking up. I didn't want to be pigeonholed into being a Democrat or a Republican, so I registered as an Independent, but that means I can't vote in the primaries, so I'm re-registering. I'm doing all kinds of new things I never would have done before. Like I went on that march in Washington. The pro-choice march. It was exhilarating. Helen Reddy sang I Am Woman. I freaked. I'm such a dyke sometimes, and I don't even have lesbian tendencies ... Go figure. I mean I feel politically that I could be lesbian, but I'm not attracted to women. There you have it. My life is full of contradictions but the march was incredible. I think it was the closest I ever got to really living in the sixties. All those people marching together for a cause. You could feel the energy. You know I met a few people in these rooms who were active drinkers and users during the sixties and who are clean now. One of them said to me that all the love and peace they were talking about and looking for, they found in these rooms ... you know, I know what they mean. I can still be Janis Joplin of the Holiday Inn circuit if I want to be. I'll just be her, alive and sober. You get me talking and I can't stop. Thanks. That's it.

(JIM jumps in after DEBBIE's last word.)

JIM. Hi my name is Jim, and I am an alcoholic.

ALL. Hi Jim.

JIM. Debbie I get angry when I hear people talk about the program like you just did. I'm sorry I'm not saying you made a joke of it, but I get angry when I hear people talk about AA like it's some fad or some fancy social club. This fucking disease ate up half of my life. More than half. It's not a joke. You see some people check in and out of here like it's a fucking hotel. I take this program seriously. It saved my live. I'm not taking anybody's inventory. I know each person has their own process of recovery, but I get mad when I hear people making fun of it. They had this whole big thing on TV about the rage of sobriety. I hope more people are getting sober. I just want people to know it's not the "in" thing to do. It's not like joining the Glee Club. For most people, it's a life and death situation. I see younger and younger people coming in here getting sober, and I'm happy for them, but way down deep inside I'm jealous ... I'm jealous of them because they're getting help early. I know it's selfish, but it's true. I wish I came in here twenty years ago. Then I could have given more good years to my wife. She deserved it. Don't get me wrong. I am happy for these kids. I'm just angry at myself, that's all. I want more of everything. More. More. I want more time with my wife. I think that's why I'm feeling all this anger. I feel like God has forgotten about me. He betrayed me. This is my first Christmas without my wife. Last year at this time, we were getting ready to go out for a pre-Christmas dinner. Don't get me wrong. God has been good to me. He gave me five good years with my wife. Sober years. If you think I'm an asshole now, you should have seen me when I drank, but she put up with it all. Good times and bad times. She was so happy when I got sober. It was like we had a new chance at life. She was a victim of alcoholism, and she didn't even drink. All those years of my drinking. She was miserable. She couldn't get control of her life. She later told me she thought about leaving me many times, but she didn't know where to go ... or what to do. She felt useless. Besides, she said, "Who would have taken care of you!" She's right. I would have died without her. She was co-dependent. When I came to AA, she went to Al-Anon, and we both began our recovery from this disease. I learned that you didn't have to drink to be affected by this disease. I have the same war stories as all of you: the fights, broken windows, jail, whoring around. She put up with it, and when I got sober, she forgave me for all of it. I became a puppy with her. I couldn't lover her enough. After I got sober, I fell in love with you all over again. I couldn't be around her enough. We were like teenagers in love. We spent all our time together. We didn't need anybody else. We were inseparable. I used to say to her on a Saturday night, "You wanna go out?", and she'd say, "No, let's just stay in and watch TV." We didn't need anybody else. We'd lie there and just enjoy each other's company. She became my best friend. I didn't have drinking buddies anymore. Now I don't have her, but I have this fellowship. I guess the anger comes from hurt and fear. Fear of the unknown. What happens to me now? I miss her so much. After work, when I open the door to my house, I expect to see her. I miss touching her, surprising her with little gifts, taking our Sunday walks up Columbus Avenue. Eating with her. Talking to her and, most of all, laughing with her ... everything ... we were partners ...

partners in life ... she went fast. She had cancer. I used to help her with everything, and when she was in the hospital, she was pretty bad. She asked me to help her ... It was the one time I couldn't do anything for her. I couldn't help her. I was powerless ... I was there when she went, and I couldn't do anything to save her. Her eyes were straining. They were looking at me as if they were saying, "C'mon, get me out of here. You've always taken care of me before. Get me out of here." I wish I could have done something, but I couldn't. I wish I was better to her in the years that I drank. She deserved it ... When she went, I took her little body in my arms and I started shaking her, asking her "Why" Why?" I lost it. I was screaming at God, asking Him, "Why? Why did you have to take her when things were just getting good. Why did you wait til I got sober? Why now? Why not when I was drunk? Why did you help me get sober and then pull the rug? My partner. I HATE YOU GOD. WHY?! TELL ME!!" I want to know why God took her. A good woman. Everybody loved her. Nobody had a bad word to say about her. Why her and not some drug addict. Why her and not some bum in the street. You ever take a look at some of these guys. They look like they got every disease in the book, but they're still going strong. Why did he help me get sober to lay this shit on me?! This priest I was getting counseling from told me to get this book called When Bad Things Happen to Good People. To tell you the truth, I had to do everything in my power to hold myself back from hitting him right in the fucking face. I haven't had these violent feelings in a long time. They're dangerous to me. I'm mixed up. I've been searching for those answers, too. I don't hate God anymore. I just don't understand, but I'm trying. I'm so mad inside I could just spit.

I'm sorry. I'm usually not so ... such an asshole. I just feel like I have my head on backwards. It's Christmas, and I feel miserable ... and the last few Christmases have been great. Last year, we went and saw them light the tree in Rockefeller Center and then went ice skating. We were like kids together. Discovering this new life in sobriety. We decorated the apartment. She fixed it up great. I can't tell you the feeling I have inside. I can't explain it. Why do I think nobody has ever loved like this before? I went to group therapy with some people who lost their loved ones. They say time will heal all wounds ... I just don't see it happening. I just don't see a future without her in my life. Some guy on my job told me to go to Cancun and get sun and find some babe. I almost punched him in the face. Another guy who lost his wife a few years ago and recently remarried told me to have a few drinks and relax, it'll all get better. I don't think these guys loved their wives the way I did. I don't want anybody else in my life. I try to keep busy now. Work as much as I can, because my apartment has become a prison to me. If I sit in it too long, I start climbing the walls. Everywhere I look, I see her. Things of hers. I still haven't gone through her closet. It's hard for me to accept that she's not here. Still, sometimes I get up in the middle of the night to go to the bathroom, and I'm real quiet because I think she's lying beside me, and I don't want to wake her, and then I look beside me and she's not there ... the bed's empty and the sheets are cold ... and I feel this dark emptiness inside, and from somewhere inside me, I hear, *(He whispers)* "She's gone." What I miss most about her is her companionship ... I can't tell you how lonesome I am. It hurts me to have to sit here and say that to you. I always thought of myself as indestructible. Here I am this big man who is self-destructing. I'm trying to hold on. I'm trying to be sane, but it's hard. The truth is I've even thought about suicide, but I'm too much of a coward to do it. That could be a blessing. The one thing that keeps me going is my faith. I know it's true, that one day we'll be together again. That she's waiting for me. Somehow this all fits into God's plan. I don't know how, and I definitely don't agree with it, so I turn it over. I'm tired of being angry and sad and pitying myself. The reason I'm talking is I'm trying to rid myself of it. I really had to look over the steps again. And I did the third step over and over. I made the decision to turn my will and my life over to the care of God, as I understood him ... it helps me. Not all the time, but some time. I know that God didn't love me but I left him, I wish we had more TIME. Don't get me wrong. I know in the five sober years we had together, we did more things and had more fun than most people do in a lifetime, but still it doesn't seem enough. Sometimes I just wish I would have made love to her more. I wonder if she knew how much I love her. I had some good days, but it seems like tomorrow is never going to get here. Sometimes I feel like what's the point. I work to make money, to spend it on who? I don't need anything. Lately I've gotten into this weird habit of reading the obituaries. I read who the deceased has left behind and I feel this immediate bond towards them. I feel like calling them, but I don't. I just don't think they'd understand how I feel. I feel myself drawn to people telling stories of loss, like a moth to light. I guess there is some truth to that saying "Misery loves company". I keep saying that after Christmas I'll be fine, but Christmas is just another day like any other. After Christmas, I'll have to get through Tuesday, then Wednesday, then New Year's Eve, then it'll be the second, then February ... I just have to get through it all. I never felt fear like this before. The fear of getting old alone. We used to go to Atlantic City all the time. She loved playing the slot machines. She got tennis elbow from it once. We used to take walks along the boardwalk, and when we saw old couples together, we'd joke around and say, "That's us in 20 years." This cute little old couple walking hand in hand, and now it's no longer us. It's just me. I was never afraid to be alone before. She used to take care of everything for me. I never used to worry about who would take care of me if I was sick, and now I have to think about things like that. She took care of all our bills ... everything. I never used to worry about who would take care of little things ... and I find myself worrying now over dumb things ... I don't know. I hope you don't think I was being a hard ass before ... I'm usually not ... I'm just mixed up. We did have a few good hears ... I'm staying sober, too ... I wouldn't shame her ... I'm doing it for me, too. You know, I got a Christmas card from this couple we met on a trip. Her name was in it. They didn't know she died ... it busted me up. I'm going to make sure her name and her spirit always live in me as long as I can speak. On my first year anniversary of sobriety, my wife gave me a card. In it, she wrote, "We'll be together till the end of time." I wanna say, "Honey, I can't wait." A friend of mine said, "You should write a book." I said, "It's easier to buy one." Thanks for listening. Merry Christmas from an old hard ass and his wife, Kathy.

JACK. Thanks, Jim. *(HELEN has her hand raised)* Helen.

HELEN. Hi, my name is Helen, and I'm an alcoholic.

ALL. Hi, Helen!

HELEN. Hi! I'm shaky today ... my mind is playing tricks on me. I don't want to talk but I want to talk, you know what I mean ... I know I need to. I want to laugh. It's just nerves. I used to answer phones in a sex club. And that's on my mind today. I guess you could say I'm a success story. I used to take the reservations during the day. I had to memorize this sales pitch. I answered the phone, and I had to say, "Hello, M.I. – Midnight Interlude – may I help you, please? I'll give you some information about our club. Yes, yes. We are a swing club. Open to single men, single woman and couples. It is $80.00 for single men, $30.00 for couples and $5.00 for single women. That fee includes a hot and cold catered buffet dinner, large open bar, shower, locker room facilities and a large open orgy room sex area for your pleasure. We do not guarantee that you have sex, but there is a good chance. Right! The ratio of men to women varies throughout the night." What I was really saying was good luck, buddy, in trying to get laid. It was sort of like Plato's retreat with prostitutes. I got the job through the Village Voice. The prostitutes – I'm gonna call them the girls – call in to see if they were working that night. Every night it would vary on how many girls we needed, according to how many reservations we had for single men. So the girls would call in and I would tell them if they were confirmed for the night, or if they were on stand-by, or that they should call back. I sort of felt like I was working at the airport. I mean, I wasn't one of the girls, I just answered phones. Sometimes I cooked. They had that buffet. I just helped run the place. Sometimes I had to put the sheets on the mats in the orgy room. Other times I had to keep score on the girls. That was the hardest job. The staff used to rotate its positions at night. So whenever I worked at night, I always tried avoiding keeping score. Let me explain what keeping score meant. You had to stand in the back of the orgy room and watch everybody. The owner gave you this card to keep score. The card had each girl's name printed on it with boxes next to the names to place their points in. The card was called the I.B.M. card, also commonly known at the club as the Intercourse, Blowjob and Masturbation card, and you had to keep track of who did what. I and B need no explanation, but M meant if a girl got more than two guys to get off at the same time and start a scene, then she got an M which meant more money. Depending on how many guys the girls did, their salary varied. Whenever I kept score, I always gave the girls lots of extra points. They would walk by me and whisper, "Thanks." The owner would always corner me and say, "Are you sure she did that many?" Absolutely, positive, I'd say. I was always drunk at this job. I drank all day answering the phones. Sometimes I'd invite friends over during the day, take the phones off the hook and party. The reservations truly depended on my drinking. If I was in a good mood, and sober, they got a lot of reservations. This was a foolproof job. Any moron could have done it, but not me. I got fired not once, not twice, but three times from it. They kept hiring me back, with one condition. That I stop drinking. I couldn't do it. Every time I was left alone, I'd hit the liquor cabinet. Finally, they put chains on it. I know it must be hard to believe, but the owners were good to me. I don't know what I would have done for a job if they didn't take me back. If I had any self-esteem, I would have quit, but I really didn't think I could do anything else. I was getting paid $5.00 an hour off the books with all the liquor I wanted, and sometimes an added benefit of drugs. Every time they fired me, I begged for my job back. I'm a college graduate, a woman in her thirties, and I was changing sheets in a sex club for a living. That's where drink got me. I had so many blackouts there. It was like working in a circus there, like I was working in a freak show. I saw everything. I worked there for quite a while. It got to the point where sex disgusted me. Men, in particular, for a while. I mean, everybody knew the girls were working there. They weren't swinging females. There were some couples who came regularly got into it, though. Some of the regular men acted as if they were in grade school. If one of the girls wasn't paying enough attention to them, they would come up to the front desk and say, "Chanel isn't being very friendly tonight." And I felt like saying, "Maybe she hates your fucking guts." But I wouldn't, unless I was drunk. I'd usually say, "Maybe she's not in a very good mood" – with a fake smile. This is my first year of sobriety, and it's been rough. I don't even have a year yet. I have six months. I'm thinking about that club, because that's where I spent last Christmas Eve. Working. Drinking. For some reason, I feel like a failure today. I feel like I should be ahead. My sponsor keeps telling me I am ahead, but I don't see it. All I know is that I'm not drinking. My sponsor says that's enough ... uhh ... *(This is hard for her to say)* Last Christmas Eve, I woke up on those mats ... I was naked. I heard myself laughing, and I opened my eyes. There were these naked men touching me. One was inside me. I felt this man's beard against my thigh. The girls were laughing, standing in the back. I began to cry. I got my stuff together and left. I never went back. I quit. I guess I'm not such a failure ... do any of you ever feel like you're not going to make it? I mean it's just a glass or can with liquid in it. Why can't I control it? So many people do ... why is it so powerful? Somewhere way in the back of my mind, I think that someday, somehow I'm gonna be able to control it. I'll be able to just have a few drinks and walk away from it. I know that's the wrong way to think ... I just want to say to Jim, I have a hard time with men, and I'm glad I heard you tonight, because it reminds me there are some good men out there ... Your wife was very lucky to have you, Jim. You're not such a hard ass ... I'm just at the beginning of something. I know it. I hear how grateful a lot of you are, and it makes me look forward to having a couple of years under my belt. I just hope I'm here next year at this time, because the last time I got really drunk – blackout drunk – I woke up in a hospital on a suicide attempt. I did my wrists. I used a razor blade. I don't remember doing it, but I remember feeling shaky, like the way I've been feeling lately. Everything is heavy. Every day life just seems to overwhelm me. The simplest things, like going outside to shop for food, cause me great anxiety. I begin to shake. I cry. I try not to let anybody know how I'm feeling, so I make up jokes about everything. I'm hiding. I try and laugh it all off ... I don't know ... I'm here ... *(She shakes her head and puts her head down)* I know I'm at the beginning of something, but I just don't know if I can make it. I don't feel good inside. I keep seeing myself at that club ... the men ... the mats. Today I don't feel any better than the first day I walked in here. Right now, more than anything in the world I just want to drink. I want to drink ... I want to drink. I know it's my choice ... but I need it. I don't think I'm gonna make it. Me sitting here is really just a bunch of horseshit. What's the purpose? I want to be sober, yes, I want to be strong, but I'm not strong like the rest of you. I'm lying right now. I picked up yesterday. I smoked a joint and drank. I had to. I had to get through it. It helped me. I only had one. I didn't black out. I just needed the one, just to calm me down. You probably don't understand. I was gonna drink this afternoon, but I came here instead. I'm trying. I can't keep running here every time I'm gonna use. I can't keep hiding in these rooms ... it keeps finding me. When none of you are around. I'm not like the rest of you. I can't do it. I'm not as strong. I'm scared that when I walk outside of this room, I'm gonna walk straight into a bar. I'm here because I want you to stop me. I don't think I can do it. I'm sorry. Stop staring at me like that!

(HELEN gets up and storms out of the room.)
(Blackout)

RACHEL. Hi, my name is Rachel, and I'm an alcoholic and a drug addict.

ALL. Hi, Rachel.

RACHEL. Hi. I'm really very happy to be here to hear you speak, Jack. All of you, really. I identify with bits and pieces from all of your stories ... um ... I guess we're all not so different from one another, but when I was drinking, I thought I was. Not only different but better. I remember one of my girlfriends once said to me, "Why do you always insist on being so special. Why don't you just relax and sit back and be ordinary like everybody else?!" She was right. That really hit me, you know ... I was trying too hard to be somebody, and with my drinking, I was achieving being a very busy nobody. I was an only child. I kept begging my parents to have another child, but they didn't ... they did the right thing, though. Why screw up two little kids when you could do it to one. I wanted a little sister or brother, a little baby to play with so bad. I told my mother I was going to have a large family when I got married. I wanted lots of babies. I've always loved kids. I babysat a lot when I was younger so I could be around them. That was before I drank. I always had this feeling I'd be a good mother. I took great care of my dolls ... I ... uh ... I always made sure they looked perfect. I made clothes for them and everything. Even in my business, I have this maternal instinct to new girls just starting out. I try to guide them, give them some advice. I wish someone did that for me. I started modelling at a very early age, and I became very successful too quickly. I drank before I got into modeling, too. I drank with my girlfriends when I was about fifteen. They all got sloppy and out of control, but I didn't. I handled it. I handled the booze, and I prided myself on that. I didn't realize that that was going to be one of my big weaknesses in life. I controlled it. Control has always been a big issue in my life. Anyway, I liked it. I liked the way it made me feel. Then I got into drugs. I started with hash and worked my way up. Of course, eventually I lost control of my drinking and drug use. I was always told to be a lady, and as my drinking progressed, I wasn't. My father is an alcoholic. He just celebrated 15 years. My mother is a very serious borderline alcoholic. Very borderline. Serious! They're divorced now, but I grew up watching them drink all the time. I thought I was the reason they drank. I didn't know if it was my fault or not. Somehow I felt I was to blame for their drinking. I grew up in that kind of volatile home life where you didn't know what was going to happen next ... I wanted to be Daddy's Little Girl ... and sometimes I was. There's a very special relationship. I don't think anybody really understands it. Between a father and a daughter. The only one who really understands it is them. I was allowed to drink beer when I was fifteen. It was a normal thing in my house. It was like, you want a soda or a beer? Sure, I'll take a beer! It was no big deal. I knew my father drank too much, but I didn't know what alcoholic meant. My mother enabled him. She covered up for him. They both were sleeping around. It was a very unhealthy environment for a child to be raised in. A major dysfunctional family. I remember one of my first times getting drunk. I felt free. I was usually so inhibited. So careful not to rock the boat, because if I did, then one of them would drink, and I didn't want that. I remember feeling free to do anything I wanted to. I could laugh. I could cry. I could not be a lady if I wanted to. I just felt free. Right away I knew I liked the feeling alcohol gave me ... It's hard for me to admit that my mother wasn't a very loving woman, but she wasn't. My family wasn't a happy family, no matter how much I want to make believe they were. When anybody asks me how my childhood was, I always say, "Great, happy. Fine, just fine.", but the truth is, it wasn't. I wanted it to be, but it wasn't. My family is emotionally constipated. I grew up believing I should not discuss my feelings. My mother said it was too American. Too ugly. She was born in England. To this day, she doesn't talk about her feelings at all. If something gets too close to home, she changes the subject. So I learned not to discuss my feelings with anybody. I ... ah ... bottled up everything inside. I buried my feelings in drink. I just swallowed them and stuffed then into my stomach ... way down in my stomach. I used to get this pain. My way of releasing any kind of emotion or family insanity was through drink. She told me if I ever told anybody about our family problems, I would be betraying her. That I would be disloyal to our family. So I was loyal for a long time and drank. I learned that through drinking and drugging, I could change my state of being. I could alter my state. I hated being in a normal state. It was just uncomfortable for me. So I changed it. I didn't have to feel the pain I was going through. It seemed to make everything easier. It was an easy way out. All an illusion. Right after my parents' divorce, I went to Paris. I wanted to get away from both of them. In Paris, my drinking really took and so did my modeling career. I was making all kinds of money. I was on every cover. At first I drank good, expensive wines. You know, like a nicè '82 Bordeaux, or a light Chardonnay. Then when I really got into it, it didn't matter. I started getting big jugs of Folonari. That's when I drank alone in my room ... I couldn't taste the difference. It all tasted alike to me ... I drank alone a lot. I was really lonely, even though I was being taken out all the time, and I was at all these parties. I was successful and lonely. A useless combination. I could handle a lot of liquor. I knew I could probably drink whoever I was going out with under the table, and that's a bit too macho for a high fashion model – for the image I was trying to present as a model – so I would drink at home before I met whoever I was meeting so when I got there, I was feeling no pain, but I could deal. I started needing the alcohol in order to be with people. I couldn't be around people sober. I just couldn't do it. I didn't ... I would be whoever you wanted me to be, but I could only be that person until the alcohol or drug wore off. Then I was nobody. I remember listening to Neil Young singing some song. You know his voice? It's sad. I identified so much with that sound of his voice. I felt lonely inside like he sounded. Drugs insulted me. I pretended to be whatever I thought you would like. I was this little girl, living like a woman. I look the part, I pulled it off. I must have known I was killing myself with the drugs and alcohol, because I became a health food nut. A maniac. Proteins, amino acids, all kinds of vitamins, and I'd wash them down with a drink. Unconsciously, I think I was trying to save myself. At the same time I got into health food, I got into cocaine. I was back in New York by now. Cocaine became my drug. I started smoking cigarettes, too, and working out at my health club at the same time. I was a walking contradiction. I was really pissed off at myself, too, because I had sworn to myself I would never smoke cigarettes, but you know when you do coke, you gotta smoke, and you have to drink wine, because you gotta have that balance. Right? I would sit up at night by a lamp, cooked out of my mind, reading HEALTH BOOKS, because I wanted to maintain my looks. Right. Because I was modeling. That's how I made my money. I was going nuts. I would do cocaine wearing mudpacks. I didn't date people for any length of time. I met this one guy I was crazy about, but it didn't work out. Alcohol was a jealous lover. There was this excitement about alcohol I was addicted to. For a while, there was this concept I had ... I thought alcohol was romantic or something ... I remember I used to take long hot bubble baths and have a bottle of champagne right at my side and a little Marilyn Monroe mirror to cut my lines on. I loved that ritual. There was something almost erotic about it ... almost ... I don't know. Since I got sober, I almost never take a bubble bath. It's funny. I miss them. You know what I mean, it's like ... you shower, you get in, you shower. You have things to do, places to go, people to meet. Then it was like this illusion for me. You know, the bubbles, the champagne, the crystal, the coke. Then, I liked reading ... I don't know, poetry or some shit. The phone was always in the room, too. If my story sounds a bit hazy, that's because that's how my life was. It's all a bit hazy in my mind. After a while, I started getting a bad name in the business. I was beginning to look awful. I would show up for jobs with my eyes bugging out of my head from all the coke. I'd watch the first Mary Tyler Moore show, the first one. That came on about two a.m., then I'd swear to myself that I'd go to bed after the second show. That was when Mary Tyler Moore was on really late, but then I'd wind up doing more lines and I'd clean my house and just watch the sun come up. It's a very lonely feeling when you know the rest of the world is asleep and there you are alone snorting away, watching the sun come up alone. Then Linda Ellerbee would come on. I think she would, anyway. My agent told me basically she couldn't represent my look anymore, which is what I always say is the drunken bum look. I looked really shabby. It was at the point where I had to have a drink. I was hiding bottles in my apartment, hiding my drinking from my friends. I didn't know what to do with my life. It came to the point where there was nothing I could do but stop drinking ... and that was just out of the question. My life had become unmanageable. All the liquor stores in my neighborhood knew me. This one guy at this liquor store said to me, "You go through this stuff like water!" And he was only getting a fifth of my business ... Cocaine really helped me drink. Ha. It kept me awake so I could drink longer. One night I was coked up and I ran out of booze. It was about four in the morning. I was in a semi-blackout. My apartment was dry and I needed a drink. I went from floor to floor in each incinerator room to see if anybody had left any bottles with just a drop in it. That's all I needed. A drop. I was desperate. I found these two bottles of Budweiser with some suds in them. They were in the garbage room. I got them, brought them back to my apartment, filled them halfway with water and shook them up and drank them. I just wanted to get that taste. It's funny but I never liked beer. It never dawned on me that I could go downstairs to some deli and get a six-pack, but after that night, whenever I got in a jam, I did. This was close to the end of my drinking, but it wasn't my bottom yet. The mixture of coke and alcohol was almost lethal for me. One night I had gotten into an argument with a friend and I jumped into my car and headed out to Long Island. I got into an accident ... thank God I didn't hurt anybody but myself. I broke my pelvis in three different places. It was on the LIE. I was wearing sunglasses. It was one o'clock in the morning. I was tired. I was three quarter miles from the midtown tunnel. I was going pretty fast, and I kind of fell asleep at the wheel and I went into a cement divide. I split my head open ... and I lied to everybody. I said someone was chasing me. Some guy with a souped-up car. You know, with wheels higher in the back. I made up this whole story about how he cut me off and just took off. I didn't want to be responsible for it. Well, that just isn't true. I lied. I caused it. I created the whole thing myself. I was responsible for the accident. I can't believe, but even that didn't stop me. I made a joke about it. I said, "Maybe it's God's way of telling me to slow down," but it didn't slow me down. It gave me the perfect reason to stay in bed and drink. And I did. I lay in bed and recuperated and drank. I was lucky. I came out of that car accident alive.

Because of drunk driving, many people each year are killed in car accidents, or disfigured or paralyzed. Their whole lives are completely altered because of it. Usually another innocent party is killed or hurt, because of someone's drinking. I could have been stuck in a wheelchair for the rest of my life, so I know I'm lucky. After a few more months of drinking like that, I finally reached out for help. That's when I hit bottom. I knew my father had gotten help with his problem with alcohol. I hadn't spoken to him in years. And I knew he was recovering, whatever that meant. I knew he wasn't drinking. I didn't know how or anything like that, and I phoned him, and I said, "Dad, how do you live without drinking. I mean how ... how can you do it?" He was really great about it. I mean he ... he ... I don't remember exactly what he said to me, but he said, "I'll help you!" He had been sober for quite a while by then. He made arrangements for me to go to a rehab in California. He got me a plane ticket and said he'd pick me up at the airport. I have vague memories of that flight. The trip is a blur to me, because I knew when I got there, I was going to have to stop drinking, so I drank everything in sight. I had that stewardess running up and down that aisle. Somehow I made it off the plane alive. God knows how, and I came out of a blackout, going around the conveyor belt with the luggage. One of those rubber straps that the luggage comes through smacked me in the face. There I was, sitting with my feet up and my hands wrapped around my legs like this. I must have gone around several times, because some of the other passengers were laughing and waving at me. Suddenly I saw my father. He just looked at me and he said, "Hi, Rach. C'mon, let's get out of here." He helped me off. Daddy's little girl. I mean, here I was this grown woman coming out of a blackout, wondering, "What am I doing on this conveyor belt? Why am I the only one on here? Where's my father?" He was right there for me. I remember I said to him, "I was looking all over for you!" Right. All over. He didn't say a word about it. He didn't blink an eye, like it was normal. The rehab didn't work. I wasn't ready for the commitment. I thought I was going to La Costa. I packed bikinis and halter tops. I was out of control, but I was OK ... right. I remember my dad walked me to my room in the rehab, holding my hand, and it felt wonderful. I remember that moment so well. I was scared and my daddy was taking care of me. While I was away for a while, I told people I was taking care of this hypoglycemic problem. I drank as soon as I got out. I didn't believe that alcohol was such a potent, powerful thing. So I began to test myself. I would take a sip of a drink to see if I would turn into Dr. Jekyll or Mr. Hyde or what's gonna happen, and nothing happened and nobody was looking, so I drank. I was just educated about alcoholism, but I didn't believe it. I just wasn't ready to make that commitment. I wasn't ready to admit that I was powerless over alcohol. Within a month, I was back in rehab and this time, I did it. I listened. I obeyed. I was sober. Life in sobriety has been good to me. I'm not saying I don't have hard times now. I do. But as long as I'm sober, I know I have a fighting chance. Sobriety has been a long process for me. I just started dealing with my character defects. First I was just staying sober and going to meetings and then that wasn't enough for me. I wanted to work on my alcoholic attitudes and feelings. Alcoholism is a disease that affects the mind and body and the soul. It is also a disease of your spiritual life. I started developing my spiritual life, which is a very important part of my sobriety. I've been married now for four years, and I love it. Ever since we've been married, Kenny and I have been trying to have a baby, and it hasn't happened to me. I've been through a lot of surgery and stuff, and I'm angry, because I want a baby more than anything. I'm angry with myself, because I think it's my fault. I still believe that ... you know, it could be a number of things ... but, you know, that car accident ... I fractured my pelvis in three places. I did a lot of fucking damage to my body. You know I took a lot of drugs. I never thought of the consequences. I mean all I've ever wanted was to have a baby. You know, I was doing all this abuse to my body at that time ... I never thought it would take away my chances of having a baby. It's the one thing I want more than anything. I believe I did the damage, but ... I don't know ... but that's what I have to live with for the rest of my life ... I feel like I'm being paid back for what I did before. I wish I didn't have any regrets, but I do. I'm not going to stop trying. I don't want to believe I made myself infertile. When I drank, I never thought about the future. My children ... I don't know what to say ... life's hard. I want to shut the door on my past ... I don't know. The most valuable lesson to me is that people share their feelings. I mean ... I really didn't know that. That's been my saving grace. I mean, we go to these rooms and we share our feelings. I realize now it's OK to have feelings. That it's OK to feel bad. It's not the end of the world to feel bad, you know, but to experience your feelings and go through them instead of always trying to numb them and stuff them way down into your stomach. That's ... I'm learning how to live ... that's it. Maybe some people can't identify with my infertility problems, but the pain is the same. You know, I went out and I got a little

Christmas stocking, and I hung it over the fireplace. I marked it "Baby". I filled it with little toys and candy. When you go home tonight, would you do me a favor? Keep me and my husband in your thoughts. Pray for us, that maybe next year at this time we'll have a little baby to give it to. We're not going to stop trying. Besides, trying is fun. I don't know. We'll see. I'm just happy I'm sober and I have a fighting chance. Pray for us. Things are hard, but I'm OK. I'm a survivor. Helen, you say you want us to stop you, but we can't stop you. We can help you, but we can't stop you. OK ... Be good to yourself. Don't pick up, just for today.

    BECKY. Hi my name is Becky and I'm an alcoholic.

    ALL. Hi, Becky.

    BECKY. I'm here today because I'm grateful. I hear a lot of people blaming their drinking on their parents. I can't do that. It wasn't that way with me. I was lucky. My parents were great. They were supportive, loving. They were always behind me one hundred percent, in everything I did. It was me. I take all responsibility for all of my drinking. No one forced me to drink. No one picked up the glass and put it to my mouth. It was my decision. I take all of the responsibility. I'm angry at myself because I did it, but I did it. No one else. I heard one guy say, "I don't blame my parents, but it was their fault." That's the wrong way of thinking. I can't blame it on anybody but myself. My parents were both great people. They didn't drink. I wasn't abused. They loved me and they showed me that all the time. I was the one who fucked up. After hearing some of your stories, I feel like my life hasn't been that bad. My bottom wasn't that bad, but for me it was. I guess it's all relative. I don't have time to go into all the details. I didn't lose my job. I didn't go to a detox. I didn't lose my husband. I almost did, but I didn't. I didn't have sex with strangers. OK, maybe once or twice. No, but you know what I mean. No, I didn't! I've always been a pretty faithful person. Even when I hit bottom in 1989, I was making $100,000.00 a year! Don't repeat that. The IRS will kill me. Just kidding. No, my bottom was more like how I was affecting my family. In particular my husband and my daughter. I remember close to the end of my drinking, my husband threatened to leave me and take my daughter. He said I wasn't the person he married. He was right. I wasn't. It started out just a few cocktails after work with the girls. I'm a business woman. Wine at lunch. Then wine at dinner. Some cognac to relax in front of the fireplace at home. I thought I was a social drinker. I think I began as one, but then it got out of hand. I didn't have my first drink until I was 22 years old, and I didn't like it then. When all my girlfriends were getting drunk in college, I wasn't. I was a good little girl. Maybe that's why I wanted to be a bad one when I got older. At first I only drank at lunch and dinner. Then I began to drink in between lunch and dinner. Then I brought a few bottles of wine into my office in case any of my clients would want a drink. Sure. Good excuse. I started coming home later and later from work. I wasn't being unfaithful. I was just being sloppy. My daughter went through four different nannies. They all kept quitting on me. They loved my daughter, Chrissie, but they told my husband ... that they weren't crazy about me or anything. They couldn't take me <u>yelling</u> orders at them all the time. You know what? I didn't think I yelled. You know what? I think I'm lying. I did lose clients. I did yell. My work did suffer because of my drinking. I think I just realized that. No. I think I'm just admitting it. I went through quite a few secretaries also. Chrissie's last nanny stood up to me. I came home from work. It was a Thursday night and my husband was out of town. Chrissie wouldn't stop crying. She just kept crying and crying. It was driving me crazy, and I was angry because I had lost some papers at work or something and I was quite drunk from a long liquid lunch. And Chrissie was shrieking. Toomie, Chrissie's nanny, was trying to quiet her down, but she wouldn't stop. Toomie said she thought Chrissie had a fever. I said, " I don't care! Shut her up!" I was so angry, I was someone else. Toomie tried, but she couldn't. All of a sudden, I grabbed Chrissie from Toomie and I began hitting her and hitting her, and she kept screaming. I saw blood. This defenseless two year old girl. Toomie pushed me away and comforted Chrissie. She called me a drunk and a sorry excuse for a mother. She was right. I left the house and I stayed in some hotel room by myself that night and drank. I left my daughter for drink. It scares me to think what would have happened that night if Toomie wasn't there. Toomie took care of her. That was my bottom. The next day, I came here and I promised to love my daughter and not drink. I meant it. My drink was gin. I loved it. And you know what, I don't miss it today. I feel bad saying that, because so many people still have the urge to drink, but I don't, and I'm grateful for that. I wouldn't drink again if you paid me. Life's too wonderful now. My daughter just started school. My husband loves me. Business is great. I'm pregnant again! I hope it's twins. I have the best friends in the world, and it's all because I came here one day instead of going for a drink. Life just keeps getting better and better. I'm feeling so good. This is going to be the best Christmas ever. I've bought Chrissie so many toys this Christmas, "Toys 'R' Us" asked me if I wanted to come on staff! I'm having fun. I'm enjoying my life. I'm thankful for everything.

(Blackout)
(Lights up on KENT speaking. HELEN enters the room and stands quietly in the back.)

KENT. I'm here today because I'm feeling pretty good lately, and I want to keep it that way. So, I mean, I thought I'd plug into a few meetings, before things started going bad (you know what I mean). So, I'm trying to change that ... The biggest change in my life since I got sober is that I don't feel crazy on a daily basis ... anymore. Don't get me wrong, I still feel crazy, but not as much ... all the time ... or anything. I still have this incredible bad temper, but I'm working on it, at least I don't feel violent anymore. I get pissed off about stupid things now. Like, I'm getting married next month and ... and, and ... and I always dreamed that when I got married my family would be the perfect average American family, and now that's impossible, because the perfect average American family is Japanese ... I know it's stupid, but it really pisses me off. They just have too much money ... There is just no comparison for the way my life is today to the way it was when I drank. My values are different, even my problems are different. The truth is basically, I don't have any problems, but being human as I am, I invent them. I guess life would be too boring without them. I mean, I work myself up over some strange things ... Like the Japanese thing. It's dumb. I have a lot to be thankful for. I know the real thing that's ticking me off isn't actually the Japanese, but the simple fact that I don't own a Mitsubishi or a Toyota, and I want to. Badly. And I understand where that's coming from on a whole other level. I understand the machine behind it that makes it work ... and everything. The solution is I'll save up and buy one. Simple enough. First things first ... Let's see ... I like my future in-laws. Thank God my worries seem to be global rather than personal. My life is going so well, I can actually stop and care about what's going on in the rest of the world and try to do something about it, even if it's just my name on a petition. I'm trying. It's a good place to be. You know when I was drinking, I used to think that I was the center of the universe. That the world revolved around me. I'm trying not to think that way anymore. I'm trying to give back all the good stuff I was given. You could say I'm trying to twelve-step the world. I think what's made me so conscious of the earth's problems is that I'm really looking forward to having children. I can't wait to have my first son or daughter, and I want this world to somehow be preserved for them in all its wonder and beauty. I want to know I tried to help preserve it. I believe that a group of people living their lives with spiritual principles, like us, can change the world ... or at least shake it up a little, because you people changed my life. I could never go back to drinking knowing that life could be this wonderful. A.A. ruined my drinking career. It's true. The future seems to have no boundaries for me now. The possibilities are limitless. When I was drinking, this guy said to me, "Face it, people are miserable." I don't believe that ... not now. Not after what I've seen in these rooms. I believe people have this involuntary desire for bliss, and I know alcoholics find it here. Some people don't understand alcoholism and they think if you have a drinking problem, just stop! Don't drink! It's not as simple as that. It's not a question of willpower. An ˙

alcoholic can't just stop. It's a disease, and I live with that disease every day of my life. I get up every morning, and I have to face it and beat it. And I do every day, with this program. I beat it. I'm living proof that this program works. It's the only other choice for an alcoholic to turn to besides death or insanity, and I'm endlessly grateful for it. I know my Higher Power, God, the spirit, whatever you want to call it is active in my life. It's like the wind, when you're riding in the back seat of a car, and the wind blows across your face. You can't see it, but you know it's there, you can feel it, and it feels good. It's invisible, but it's there. I don't force or push my will anymore, and things turn out all right. Some people say that miracles don't happen on earth anymore, and on this Christmas Eve, I know they're wrong, because it's a miracle that I'm sober today. I'm a miracle, and all of you are miracles, too. I'm not in LaLa land. I do have some problems, but I see solutions now. I could go on and on, but I guess I should just stop and say, "Thanks." Good luck to all of you.

JACK. Thanks, Kent. I want to make an announcement. Church Street is having a Christmas party tonight. If anybody doesn't have a place to go, or even if you do have a place to go but you'd rather come with us and have fun, you can get the information from me right after the meeting. Which is now. I just want to thank all of you for being here tonight, because I needed you. Let's end with the serenity prayer.

(KATHY anxiously raises her hand. JACK calls on her. The group turns to KATHY.)

KATHY. *(Fighting to compose herself)* Hi. My name is Kathy and ... I'm an alcoholic.

ALL. Hi Kathy.

KATHY. I came here tonight ... because umm ... not knowing if I was really, ya know an alcoholic ... and stuff ... watchamacallit ... um ... But after listening to you guys, I'm pretty sure I am. I think ... or we've done a hell of a lot of the same things. Ya know, blackouts ... and everything and yada yada ... or felt the same way a lot or something ... We definitely drank a lot ... I came here ... tonight ... because *(She starts breaking down)* ... I had nowhere else to go. I didn't have a party to go to like some of you ... or friends or family to go to or a boyfriend. I'm not ritzy like some of you. I don't really have friends because I drink ... I don't have a home. I sleep at the women's shelter, because I drink ... I'm pregnant ... and I don't know what I'm going to do, but I know I need to stop drinking. And I want to be able to keep my baby. I have so much inside I need someone to give it to. That's why I'm here ... The father left me. I woke up and he was gone and that hurts. I was sleeping in a car ... He drinks ... I was sleeping in doorways and I don't want my baby like that, but I keep drinking with any money I get. I can't help it! I need help ... I'm scared. I don't know ... I'm here tonight. Who knows? I don't like to talk because I know I don't talk right. I'm done.

JACK. Kathy, drinking isn't going to help you. I haven't get all the answers for you, but personally I'd like to help you.

RACHEL. Kathy talk to me after the meeting, maybe I can be of some help.

(KATHY shakes her head.)

JACK. Kathy, you don't have to be ritzy or talk a certain

way to come to these rooms. The only thing you have to have, to come here is the desire to stop drinking, and you have that ... Okay? *(KATHY sits up and shakes her head yes.)* OK. Let's end with the serenity prayer. Merry Christmas, everybody.

ALL. Merry Christmas. *(All rise and hold hands)* God grant me the serenity to accept the things I cannot change, the courage to change the things I can and the wisdom to know the difference. Keep coming back, it works if you work it.

(Blackout)

THE END

OTHER TITLES AVAILABLE FROM SAMUEL FRENCH

DATES AND NUTS
Gary Lennon

Comedy / 2m, 3f / Interiors

This romantic comedy by the author of *Blackout* is about an animal rights activist in Brooklyn who is dumped by her fiancee for a man. Angry at the male species, she searches for Mr. Right or at least Mr. Right Now in the dating jungle of New York City. Her attempts are futile and she swears off men. When she actually bumps into the man of her dreams, the event goes unnoticed at first. When they do set out to conquer intimacy, they fight, laugh, love and dance their way into that heart shaped bed for newlyweds in the Poconos.

OTHER TITLES AVAILABLE FROM SAMUEL FRENCH

OUTRAGE
Itamar Moses

Drama / 8m, 2f / Unit Set

In Ancient Greece, Socrates is accused of corrupting the young with his practice of questioning commonly held beliefs. In Renaissance Italy, a simple miller named Menocchio runs afoul of the Inquisition when he develops his own theory of the cosmos. In Nazi Germany, the playwright Bertolt Brecht is persecuted for work that challenges authority. And in present day New England, a graduate student finds himself in the center of a power struggle over the future of the University. An irreverent epic that spans thousands of years, *Outrage* explores the power of martyrdom, the power of theatre, and how the revolutionary of one era become the tyrant of the next.

GETTING AND SPENDING
Michael J. Chepiga

Comedic Drama / 4m, 3f

A brilliant and beautiful investment banker makes illegal profits of eighteen million dollars from insider trading and uses it to build housing for the homeless. Shortly before her trial, she ferrets out the foremost criminal attorney of the era to persuade him to abandon his retirement in a Kentucky monastery to defend her. This play is about them: their struggles with themselves, with each other, with the law and with her unusual defense.

"Stirs the conscience while entertaining the spirit."
– Los Angeles Times

"An off beat, audacious comedy, well worth seeing."
– WNBC TV